Who Has Spaghetti For The Yeti?

Benjamin Lachapelle

Ben Animalia Books
Mirabel, Quebec, Canada
All rights reserved
©2021 Benjamin Lachapelle
ISBN: 979-8-5352-5013-7
1st Edition

Other books by Benjamin Lachapelle available on Amazon

The Yeti Series

How Tall is a Yeti?
How Loud is a Yeti?
Who Has Spaghetti For The Yeti?

Coming soon!

The Yeti's Footprint

This book is dedicated to
my 婆婆 (Po Po)
and 公公 (Gong Gong)

The animals are having a party.
A potluck party!

The Nene invites the Yeti.
They are friends.

"I will only come if there is spaghetti," says the Yeti.

"I only like spaghetti."

"There will be spaghetti, dear Yeti," replies the Nene.

The animals are coming.

Each bringing food to share.

A lamb brings yams.

A pig brings figs.

The bear brings eclairs.

And two mice bring rice.

The Nene brings penne.
And the Yeti…

Well, the Yeti only likes spaghetti.
Who has spaghetti for the Yeti?
His tummy is growling.

"Do you want to try the other good food?"
the Nene asks the Yeti.

"No. I only like spaghetti," replies the Yeti.

The Nene remembers
the giraffe will bring spaghetti.

These party animals keep coming.

A parrot brings carrots.

A pony brings macaroni.

The puffin brings muffins.

An antelope brings cantaloupes.

And a hungry seal brings a bowl of oatmeal.

Oh, what a feast!

A wise old moose brings some juice.

A canary brings cherries.

The wolverine brings tangerines.

A cheetah brings pitas.

And the garganey brings a big bag of candy.

This party will be fun!

But the Yeti is still waiting for spaghetti.

The Nene picks up the telephone
to call the giraffe,

"*Giraffe, are you bringing
the spaghetti for the Yeti?*"

The Yeti's tummy is growling and
grumbling.

"*No,*" answers the giraffe.

"*I do not have spaghetti for the Yeti.*

*But I think my friend the elephant
is bringing the spaghetti.*"

The guests continue to arrive.

The goldfishes bring Danishes.

The mosquitos bring burritos.

A turkey brings beef jerky.

And a cony brings baloney.

A Thomson's Gazelle brings caramel.

The Barbary Ape brings grapes.

A jacana brings bananas.

The Corn Snake brings cheesecake.

And a rainbow trout brings brussels sprouts.

This party will be great!

They are followed by a quetzal
who brings pretzels.

And a megalodon who brings wontons.

But who has spaghetti for the Yeti?

Not two leeches, who bring peaches.

And not the kiwi, who just brings kiwis.

The Yeti's tummy is growling,

grumbling and rumbling.

"Try something new while
you're waiting for spaghetti,"
the kiwi says to the Yeti.

No, the Yeti only wants spaghetti.

The Nene calls the elephant,

"Elephant, do you have the Yeti's spaghetti?"

"No, I do not have spaghetti for the Yeti," replies the elephant.

"But I think my friend the hippopotamus is bringing spaghetti."

Meanwhile…

Two blue jays bring mayonnaise.

A lioness brings asparagus.

The zebu brings honeydew.

And the Great Bustard brings custard.

This party will be **awesome**!

A pair of gannets bring pomegranates.

A Yellow-rumped Warbler

brings peach cobbler.

The kudu brings tofu.

An ostrich brings spinach.

A small Pekinese brings

a very large piece of cheese.

And a young red fox brings some lox.

A cow brings Cha Sui Boa (叉烧包).

The baboon brings macaroons.

A snail brings kale.

The oriole brings cinnamon rolls.

A halibut brings coconuts.

And the Tibetan Kiang brings lemon meringue.

This party will be amazing!

A newt brings grapefruit.

And a deer brings a pitcher of root beer.

But still no spaghetti for the Yeti.

The Yeti's tummy is growling, grumbling, rumbling and groaning.

So many snacks but the Yeti only wants spaghetti.

The Nene calls the hippopotamus,

"Hippopotamus, when will you arrive with spaghetti for the Yeti?"

"I have no spaghetti for the Yeti," the hippo replies.

"The donkey is bringing the spaghetti."

"The spaghetti is coming.

Do you want to try some of the other food?"
the animals ask the Yeti.

"It's all very yummy."

The Yeti's tummy is growling, grumbling, rumbling, groaning and moaning!

All the new foods smell very good.

The Yeti decides to try new things!
The salmon offers ramen.
And a three-toed sloth
gives him some broth.

The Yeti seems to enjoy it.

Now the Yeti is trying more new food!

WOW!

He likes all the snacks
the animals have brought!

The animals are happy
the Yeti is trying new things.

Even if he is eating up
all the food for the party!

But just then, the giraffe, elephant, hippopotamus and donkey show up with a **gigantic, enormous, humungous** plate of spaghetti.

So, it looks like it's going to be
a wonderful party after all.

Everyone will have spaghetti!
Everyone except the Yeti.

He is too full…

Well, maybe one last meatball.

About the Author

Benjamin Lachapelle, who calls himself an "Animal Knower," is a young autistic artist from the Laurentians of Quebec, Canada. He paints, sculpts, illlustrates and writes stories about animals from his unique perspective.

Benjamin is passionate about all animals and hopes to make the world more caring towards animals and a kinder place for everyone (especially those with different abilities) through his art.

Follow his work on Instagram and Facebook @BenAnimalia and view his other books on his Amazon Author's Page

Ben Animalia is a social enterprise. To inquire about creative engagements which promote animal protection, conservation, neurodiversity, autism acceptance and inclusion, please email: Ben.Animalia@outlook.com

Ben Animalia

Made in the USA
Las Vegas, NV
22 November 2022